W9-AMN-944

Scraphooks of America™

Published by Tradition Books™ and distributed to the school and library market by The Child's World®
P.O. Box 326, Chanhassen, MN 55317-0326 ➤ 800/599-READ ➤ *http://www.childsworld.com*

An Editorial Directions book
Editors: E. Russell Primm and Lucia Raatma
Additional Writing: Lucia Raatma and Alice Flanagan/Flanagan Publishing Services
Photo Selector: Lucia Raatma
Photo Researcher: Alice Flanagan/Flanagan Publishing Services
Proofreader: Chad Rubel
Design: Kathleen Petelinsek/The Design Lab

Library of Congress Cataloging-in-Publication Data

Dell, Pamela.
  Aquila's drinking gourd : a story of the Underground Railroad / by Pamela J. Dell.
      p. cm. — (Scrapbooks of America series)
Summary: In West Virginia in 1859, an eleven-year-old slave is taken from her mother and sold, dreaming of the Underground Railroad her father taught her about, but never imagining that she will board it so soon.
  ISBN 1-59187-013-5 (library bound : alk. paper)
  1. Underground railroad—Juvenile fiction. [1. Underground railroad—Fiction. 2. Fugitive slaves—Fiction. 3. Slavery—Fiction. 4. West Virginia—Fiction.] I. Title.
  PZ7.D3845 Aq 2002
  [Fic]—dc21   2002004768

Scrapbooks of America™

Aquila's Drinking Gourd
A STORY OF THE UNDERGROUND RAILROAD

by Pamela Dell

TRADITION BOOKS™
EXCELSIOR, MINNESOTA

I found these leaves during my journey to freedom on the Underground Railroad.

table of contents

"SOLD!"

The **auction** man slammed his hammer down so hard it about broke the wood of the counter he was standing behind, just off to my side. He had a voice that was hard and mean, like he was the devil's preacher up there at his very own pulpit. Spread all around in front of us and looking up was a **broadcloth** of white faces. Hateful eyes all on me. I kept all that I was feeling deep inside, making my face blank.

The auction man raised his hammer, pointed it in my direction, and said again, "Sold to Tad and Nathaniel Brockett!" My blood went icy all through my body. "A fine Negro girl slave, at a good price, too! Your

It was at an auction just like this one that I was sold away from Mama. Pappy had already been sold a while before. I knew I might never see my family again.

At auctions, slaves were shown off just like horses or cows. The men looked at our teeth, and we had to jump and prance around.

6

CAUTION!!

COLORED PEOPLE
OF BOSTON, ONE & ALL,

You are hereby respectfully CAUTIONED and advised, to avoid conversing with the

Watchmen and Police Officers of Boston,

For since the recent ORDER OF THE MAYOR & ALDERMEN, they are empowered to act as

KIDNAPPERS
AND
Slave Catchers,

And they have already been actually employed in KIDNAPPING, CATCHING, AND KEEPING SLAVES. Therefore, if you value your LIBERTY, and the *Welfare of the Fugitives* among you, *Shun* them in every possible manner, as so many *HOUNDS* on the track of the most unfortunate of your race.

Keep a Sharp Look Out for KIDNAPPERS, and have TOP EYE open.

APRIL 24, 1851.

Posters listed slaves for plantation owners to buy. We were just like livestock or other property to them.

mama's going to be mighty proud of you boys bringing her such a fine one. Come on up here, somebody, and get her!"

Rough hands grabbed me down off the block. Just as they did, my mama let out a wail so wild it was like she just lost all of everything. Like death itself just grabbed her own soul in an icy grip. She was over to the side, held fast by two **ornery-**looking white men, and was waiting to go next up for sale. Seeing me sold, she tried to wrench free, screaming my name.

"Aquila! No!" Her screaming broke down into a long sob that started one rising up from inside my own heart, too.

"Mama!" I screamed back her way. But before I could do anything but catch her eye for a last time, I was pulled off and out of there. She was gone from me forever.

Our whole family—Mama, Pappy, and me—we were like a seedpod. A pod that had been split wide open, all three of us seeds scattered every which way to the winds. Never to know which way the others went or what became of them either. Just gone. Nothing left of my heart then but an empty hole inside my chest.

Pappy had been the first to go, a month or more before. That was when Master Hemmings said that tobacco profits were way down at Oak Rest, his **plantation,** and he had to cut back some. Smaller crop this time, so not as many hands needed to work the field.

Ever since, one slave after another had gone to auction. Seemed white folks didn't care at all about a family if it wasn't white. Something was deeply wrong with that, too.

Some say that working the plantation was a **fortunate** thing. Most slaves in those parts, called western Virginia, worked the salt mines, Pappy said. Pappy knew a whole lot about things white folks didn't want a slave to know. Even knew some spelling and counting, too, which might have got him killed if the master had found out. Pappy was the one who sat me down before all this started and told me what might happen to us all. When he talked about it, his eyes were as sad as the river that kept

Most children in slave families started working in the fields at about age seven or eight, just like I did.

We slaves worked hard on tobacco and cotton plantations. Our masters expected long days from us.

us back from being free somewhere else.

He said, "Aquila, whatever becomes of us, you keep in your mind that you got a right to be free, same as anybody. Time comes, we will be, too." In those parts, everybody'd heard there were some **colored** folks who weren't slaves. And across the Ohio River, there were states where all the people were free.

My pappy filled me up with a hope for all of us. He told me everything he knew about the **Underground Railroad.** Everything he said made me strong. Kept me thinking about how to find a ride on that train someday, too.

Pappy drew a cross on the ground and said, "There are four directions you have to

Some of us called the Ohio River by another name—the Jordan River—because for us it meant freedom. In the Bible, Joshua led people across the Jordan to the Promised Land.

Western Virginia might have been a pretty spot, but it was no place for us. Our only freedom was in the Northern states or in Canada.

The Ohio River was a beautiful sight for us slaves. Across that river was freedom.

After one of those long, hot days working for our masters, we'd often sit together and sing. "Follow the Drinking Gourd" was a song that gave all of us hope.

remember, Daughter. Keep in mind that east is where the sun always comes up, and west is where it goes down. If you got the sun coming up on your right side, then you're looking north, and north is the way to the promised land."

Then he taught me about the drinking **gourd**. We sang the song, "Follow the Drinking Gourd" together, all us slaves, sitting beside the cabins after the day was done. It was a song with a secret code, taught slaves all about how to take that bitter road out of **bondage.** That was all I could think about after Pappy was gone.

As I sat in the back of a wagon on my way to someplace owned by the woman they called

Widow Brockett, my insides had a fierce burn from trying not to cry. Her sons were up front, one driving and the other just sitting like a proud, ugly rooster beside his brother. Not looking at me at all, either one, so I reached in my **satchel,** ever so quiet. I didn't have much to take along, a few rags of clothes to wear. But I had my own drinking gourd Pappy made especially for me on my eleventh birthday. That was May 17, 1859, more than a month past.

It was my very own cup for drinking from. Or maybe for keeping things in. A real gourd, dried and hollowed out. It had a smooth, golden brown color like a sunset through a haze of dust. It had a warm, hollow sound when you tapped it with your finger-

Our masters could be mighty mean to us. This little white girl tried to stop her daddy from beating his slave, but not many people ever stood up for us.

"Follow the Drinking Gourd" wasn't the only song that told slaves how to escape. "Wade in the Water" told us how to lose the dogs that might be tracking us.

We carved up gourds like these to make big drinking cups and other items. The gourds had a nice, hard skin that lasted a long time.

tips, too. Someday, when I got free from a life of do-this-and-do-that, and from getting struck or beaten if I didn't do things just right, then I hoped maybe I'd put a rose blossom in my drinking gourd. Float it in a bit of water, real pretty and sweet smelling.

Best thing of all about my birthday gift was that it had lines carved in it by my pappy himself. He took a sharp stone and carefully carved on its outsides. Carved in a shape that looks like a square cup with a long, curved handle. This was a shape of stars you can see in the night sky, what white folks call the **Big Dipper.** Us slaves knew it as the drinking

13

gourd. The cup part of the drinking gourd was outlined by four stars in a square shape. It told the secret about where freedom lies.

Pappy would point up into the dark, and we'd see that set of stars just hanging there. The drinking gourd had a powerful beauty. It glistened in the night like a promise.

"Look there, Aquila," he'd say. "You see that star, one at the corner farthest up on the bowl part, and farthest out, too? That star's your guide because it points you to the North Star, straight up above it. You see? No matter where a body stands on this ground, he sees that North Star in front of him and he knows he's facing north. It's always there to help him find his way. **Polaris** is another name for that star."

Polaris. That word had a fine, free sound to it. Pole Star. North Star. Drinking Gourd. Underground Railroad. These words ran through my head, strung together like a lullaby. Brought me a small shred of peace in the middle of all my grieving thoughts.

After they sold Pappy, his new masters took him south, a long way away, said Master Hemmings, where he'd never find his way out. Mama took sick after she heard that. Then they were both gone from me.

As the wagon carried me on to the Brockett place, I curled my arms around the drinking gourd, wishing us all back together again. I bent forward and cradled it in my lap as we bumped along the road, my eyes shut tight so no tears could ecape.

The stars in the Big Dipper looked just like the outline of a drinking gourd.
Those stars helped escaped slaves find their way north.

The only thing that put a bright spot in my head right that very minute was that the sun was setting. It cast long shadows off the side of the wagon. Dusky shadows, like we were in a funeral parade or something, stretching off to my right side. That was the only good thing about this whole procession. The sun was going down to my left, way across a wave of shiny, green tobacco leaves. We were heading north.

———

Heading north, but where we went didn't turn out to be as far as the Ohio River, like I'd been secretly wishing it to be. The wagon cut into a side road just as the land turned all to shadows. All around,

Widow Brockett's tobacco plantation looked just like this one, with rows and rows of shiny, green leaves.

The cabins we slaves lived in were small and dark. They weren't nearly as grand as the masters' homes.

Between 1830 and 1860, nearly 50,000 slaves escaped on the Underground Railroad.

things were a deep gray. The meadowlarks had gone quiet from their beautiful, joyous song, too, filling me with sadness all of a sudden. Fields on both sides had **hemp** plants growing, and up ahead I saw a house. Not so big as the big house at Oak Rest, but sizable just the same.

We pulled around back and stopped by the wide porch. Off a ways, there was a barn. Beyond that, woods. I saw two cabins, too, of rough logs, set apart and shaky looking. At Master Hemmings's place, we had nothing but dirt floors, slept on hard bunks nailed to the walls. No windows, just the door for light. I saw that was going to be my situation again.

The back door opened and out came a rail-thin woman, not too tall and with dark

Inside our cabins, we didn't have much—just a chair or two and maybe a mat to sleep on.

hair streaked gray. Behind her was a colored woman in an apron. Right away I gathered she was in charge of the kitchen business. Her lips were knit together, and there came a shake of her head when she saw me. A dark boy who'd been splitting logs by the side of the house stopped and looked up as we pulled in. He was probably only a year or two older than me, looked like.

"'Bout time you boys got back," the woman said. "Supper will be served as soon as we settle the girl." She looked over at me, and I lowered my eyes. I'd already pushed my gourd back safely in the satchel.

"She's a bargain, too, Ma," said the man who'd been driving. He stepped down off the wagon. "Looks plenty strong."

"Tad, give her some water and put her in the bin," said the woman I then knew was Widow Brockett. "I'll see to her in the morning."

She turned to the woman at her side, who was now looking sadder than I felt my own face looked.

"Get my sons' meal on the table, Lettie, and be quick about it." She looked back to me. "You there, get down out of there," she said, like she suddenly wanted to get a closer look at me. I got out of the wagon. She came down the steps and planted herself close to my face. She had a pinched look all around her features.

Right away she snatched my satchel. As quick as I could, I buried my wanting to cry out and hold tight. Widow Brockett took the satchel in three fingers like she thought it might bite or get her dainty hand full of filth. It was all clean though, just old and worn.

"What's your name, young woman?" she asked me. I couldn't tell from her yellow eyes what kind of mind she had inside that head of hers, so I was careful about every word.

"Aquila, ma'am," I replied. She did a little hummph sound out her nose.

"A biblical name," she said, and she was right. "Well, Aquila, new slaves around here we give a day or two to **acclimatize**."

"Thank you, ma'am," I said, my head bowed. I wasn't familiar with that word she spoke, "acclimatize," but I figured she meant I got to rest up. I had a gratitude feeling come up in me when I heard that.

"You follow my boy Tad now, and I don't want any fuss."

All the rest of them went back inside except the boy chopping. His eyes met up with mine as we passed him, standing there still as a picture. But when I came up close, I saw his eyes flaring with sparks, like he was angrier than a chained-up hound dog.

"Get on with it, boy, if you know what's good for you!" Tad growled as he led me toward the far end of the house. We rounded

When a lady named Prudence Crandall tried to open a school for black children in Connecticut in the 1830s, people tried to burn the school down.

the corner so I couldn't see the boy anymore but what I did see was where I was meant to be going. That thing she called the bin. It was a horror, I saw, and a scream flew out my mouth before I could stifle it. Tad slapped my face.

"Get in there!" he said, pushing me. "You hush and don't cause any trouble. A day or two, you'll be out and then you'll be ready to work, you hear?"

———

I had to bite my lips together till they nearly bled to keep from making a terrible sound. I was in near darkness, a tiny cellar room under the house, locked in. Nasty old roots were pushing out of the dirt walls like crawling hands. A little barred window just above my head was the only place to breathe air. The smell all around me was musty and **dank** enough to make me sick. I reached up and grabbed each hand around one of the bars. I lifted up on my toes to try to get a bit of the sweet night air beyond that horrible place. I breathed in and out long as I could till my feet got tired and I had to let go and stand flat again. My belly was aching for food, but there was none. I slumped on the floor of dirt and just hunched there, thinking the freedom words. The words came so strong they were like a **brand** burning into my flesh now.

Then the song came to me. In my head
it began to play, sweet and full of comfort.

When the sun comes back and
  the first quail calls,
Follow the drinking gourd,
For the old man is awaiting for
  to carry you to freedom
If you follow the drinking gourd.

All the verses after that came to me, too.
I sang them softly out loud. Pappy said they
had instructions for slaves deeper south to
get free but clues for us, too. Best to plan
your escape in springtime, the song said,
when starting out was warm. That was what
the quail and the sun signified. Birds come

P. Mazell Sculp'

The quails in "Follow the Drinking Gourd" were telling us to always plan our escapes in the springtime when the weather was warm.

back after winter, the slaves' best time to look for a ride on the freedom train.

The Underground Railroad was no real train though. Just folks, black and white both, showing secret paths out of here. Safe houses to hide in along the way.

Down in the dark and filth of that cellar, my mind hardened like an **anvil.** I didn't care about the risk. I had to get away soon as she let me out of that hole. Those were the thoughts drifting through my head while I was curled up on the ground and night grew deeper. Maybe I was sleeping, too, because all at once I jerked awake. A sound somewhere roused me, I thought, so I listened hard.

It came again.

Some brave people, like those here on Leon Coffin's farm in Indiana, helped slaves escape to the Northern states and to Canada. Some white people cared about us and didn't treat us like property.

Some people thought that "underground" meant that we escaped through tunnels, but the Underground Railroad wasn't beneath the ground at all. On the way north, we hid in barns and spare rooms and attics.

$100 REWARD!

RANAWAY

From the undersigned, living on Current River, about twelve miles above Doniphan, in Ripley County, Mo., on 2nd of March, 1860, **A NE GRO MAN**, about 30 years old, weighs about 160 pounds; high forehead, with a scar on it; had on brown pants and coat very much worn, and an old black wool hat; shoes size No. 11.

The above reward will be given to any person who may apprehend this aid negro out of the State; and fifty dollars if apprehended in this State outside of Ripley county, or $25 if taken in Ripley county.

APOS TUCKER.

Masters didn't like it when their slaves got away. Like this poster shows, they offered rewards to get us back.

"Pssst! Hey, you in there!" Just a whisper but urgent sounding. I went right to the window. There, in a sliver of moonlight, I saw his face. The wood-chopping boy. As soon as he saw me at the other side of the bars, he spoke his whisper again.

"Look, I'm getting you out of there. Keep quiet, and do all I say, you hear?"

I nodded, speechless. Fearing I was dreaming up some guardian angel and none of this was really happening. But no. He was all real. Next thing I knew, there came a quiet little scraping sound at the lock on the other side of the door. Then the door was pushed open just a bit, enough for me to squeeze out, and I did.

Suddenly I was in the night air, a swirl

of gentle wind lifting my raggedy skirt, lifting my heart at the same time. The house was all dark. Dark everywhere except for a wild sky of stars and a low **crescent** moon.

"Come on," he said. "Don't make a sound. Just follow me. And here—"

He pushed a bundle into my hands, shocked me clean through. It was my satchel. The next second, he was flying soundlessly across the back land, straight for the woods. My feet were so fast behind him that I could just as well have been running on hot coals. But it was sweet, cool grass.

The woods were blacker than a deep, dark cave, but I didn't have time to let a fear gather in me. I stumbled through behind him, pushing back branches that slapped at my face, my legs. Finally, just when I felt like I had no breath left at all and a sharp pain was ripping at my side like a knife wound, we stopped. The boy pulled me under a thick cover of vines growing out from a rocky wall, making a small, hidden space underneath.

"Just my luck you show up tonight," he said with a streak of scorn in his voice. "What's your name?"

So I told him.

"Mine's Moss," he said. "Moss grows on the north side of trees, free side."

"I know that!" I said, **huffy** on top of all

my questions. Then Moss began to answer those questions. He had picked the lock that was holding me in the bin, been practicing in secret, just in case. He'd seen where Widow Brockett set my satchel, grabbed it after she retired upstairs. Said he had a conductor coming for him just that very night. When I heard that, my heart leapt up. A **conductor** was what we call folks who took runaway slaves from one safe spot to another in the northward direction.

He wanted to leave me and just scramble off in the dead of night, Moss told me next, but said he couldn't stand the thought of one more slave buried down that cellar one more night. Then my gratefulness was so wide I had to hold back from hugging him good and tight. Couldn't think of any other way to thank him, so I just reached in my satchel and pulled out the drinking gourd. It was too dark for him to see what it was, but I placed it in his hands. Then, my voice low and hushed, I described every detail to him like we were two blind children craving for light. And I reckon we were just that.

Time passed, and he gave me a scrap of bread to eat. We didn't say anything, but the woods were loud with night creatures. The only thing that kept my fears off was grasping how, right then, I was riding the Underground Railroad, for real. Hard to imagine

Harriet Beecher Stowe wrote *Uncle Tom's Cabin*, a famous book about slavery. It helped people in the North learn about our troubles and decide to help us.

Harriet Tubman was a famous abolitionist who used to be a slave herself.
In this picture, she is on the far left, standing with some slaves she helped escape.

but true. After a bit, I heard a dog howl, far off. I grabbed Moss's arm, and he didn't try to shuck me off.

"Hush!" he said. "Tiny's coming—I hear him. Get ready now." Moss stood. Me, too. Seemed like a long, terrible time when all I heard was that braying dog. The sound seemed to get closer and closer. But suddenly the brush moved back, startling me. Then a pale face stared in at us. A pale face floating high above my head, so spooky I nearly swallowed my tongue.

"Hey, Tiny," said Moss, and I couldn't believe that his talk was so casual to a white man. A huge white man, at that.

"Hey, Moss," Tiny said back. A big smile flashed across his mouth, then disappeared into seriousness. "Got to get cracking," he said. "Who you got with you here?" Moss told him my name and the circumstances about me being along with him.

Tiny nodded. "No problem," he said. "The more, the better. But we've got to go quickly, and we've got to be quiet. Could be that Brockett mongrel we're hearing."

Tiny turned out to be the first white man **abolitionist** I ever met, even heard of by a name. Abolitionists were folks who were working to see the end of slavery forever. Abolish means to get rid of, so they were called abolitionists. I got the word from

Abolitionist Harriet Tubman was called "Grandma Moses" because, like Moses in the Bible, she helped people get to freedom.

29

Pappy, but I got the experience then from Tiny. Made me realize I was one, too. That thought drove my feet firmly through the dark of that night with no faltering. Stealing through the trees and stalked by danger, all I wanted was to go on, as fast as we could.

Tiny said we'd have to cross water as soon as we could, in case of dogs tracking our scent. He was so strong that he carried both of us a long stretch through the woods, so our footsteps couldn't be sniffed out on land either. Still carrying us, he waded across a shallow but swift-flowing stream and on up the bank a long way before he finally set us down.

In a bit, we stopped for a spell of resting. Tiny gave us some dried fruits to eat, water

Benjamin Franklin and George Washington didn't believe in slavery. They were members of the Pennsylvania Abolition Society, which started in 1787.

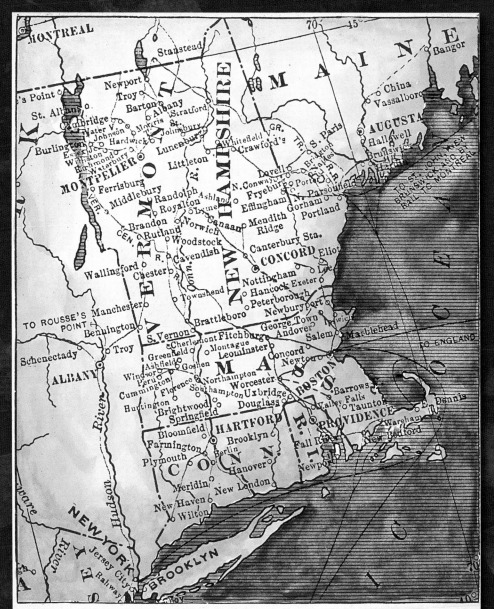

MAP OF THE UNDERGROUND RAILROAD IN NEW ENGLAND

The Underground Railroad had stops all over the northern states. These were free states, but we were safer if we made it all the way to Canada.

to drink. Then, while we rested, he filled me in about how he was a Northerner posing as a Southern man, doing handy-man work all around, wherever there were slaves. He showed us how he talked like his regular self, then how he took up talking like a Southern man. All to fool folks so they wouldn't suspect his real work, freedom work.

Moss added in, too. Said how Tiny showed up a couple months earlier, offering help on Widow Brockett's farm. Soon he started watching over Moss's own work, and after a bit they got to trust each other. That was how they started making the plan for Moss to escape. Tiny said he always left where he was working at least a month before he stole back. Then, when he'd come back to meet up with slaves he was carrying on the railroad, nobody connected that Tiny helped them go. Tiny would have been beaten or killed, too, if he was ever found out.

Just before we headed off again, Tiny took a candle from his coat and lit it up. Then he drew us a map in the dirt. Showed us that we were a ways north of Charleston, near where Widow Brockett had her farm. Showed us where we'd be going, straight to the Ohio River. But he gave us a warning. Said we had to get through a tobacco field, two more streams, and down a bit of old back road before we would get near any river at all. But when we reached the secret meeting place, he said, he'd gotten us passage across the river on a boat to a place called Gallipolis, Ohio. Ohio—a free state.

———◆———

Things went real well all through the night. Could hardly believe how well or how much awake I was either. Through the dark fields we went, rustling our way through tobacco plants. Above, the stars turned through the sky, but every time I looked up, the drinking gourd was just hanging there so

fine, pushing me onward in its direction.

We reached the river just as daylight was about to break. The sky had a pinkish streak on its eastern side. I smelled the water, too, before I ever even saw it. Seemed like the best smell I'd breathed in for a long time. Couldn't tell if I had total exhaustion or energy so high I might dance my way all the way to the water's edge. But I saw Tiny had some anxiousness in his face. He was looking quickly all around, over the back of his shoulders both ways, as we came down to the river bank. Down a bit but moving steadily in our direction came a small boat in the shadow of dawn.

William Lloyd Garrison was an abolitionist who published an important newspaper called *The Liberator*.

Sojourner Truth was another abolitionist. She was the first black woman to speak out against slavery.

It was that Ohio River that captured me though. That river looked deep and dark as a mystery. Gave a body a chilly feeling head to toe just to look at it, but I could see straight across to misty green land on the other side. The first sight of paradise I'd ever seen. In my mind came the picture of slaves walking this river all the way across in winter time, when it was frozen solid, like Pappy told me about. Some folks ran from so far south that they had far more miles to go than I did to get to this glorious spot. But I had so much gratefulness in my heart right then that I could only

Frederick Douglass was born a slave, but he escaped and worked his whole life to end slavery. He published a newspaper called *The North Star*, and his home was a stop on the Underground Railroad.

When slaves escaped, men would come after us with guns and dogs. They didn't like losing their property, I guess.

Even in the North, escaped slaves had to be careful. The only real freedom was farther north in Canada.

imagine what those other folks felt when they looked out across the water turned to a slab of ice. Where I was standing at that moment, it seemed like freedom was so close you could almost touch it and taste it.

Not quite though. In a sudden disruption of all my thoughts, **commotion** broke out. The little boat came pulling up our way. But with no warning whatsoever, gunshots fired off just back a bit in the trees, scaring me down every bone in my spine.

Tiny grabbed Moss and me by a shoulder each and shoved us hard in the boat direction.

"Run there!" he shouted. "Get on that boat! It's safe!"

"But—" I tried to hold his arm. More

gunshots fired. Then I heard the growling of dogs, men shouting.

"Go!" Tiny said, quieter in his voice, but like a firm command you can't say no to. "You'll be ferried to the other side if you make it onboard. You'll be taken to a safe house in Gallipolis. There you've got people to help you get all the way to Canada." He'd already made us understand we were only partly safe, even in the North. The only true safety was in the place called Canada.

Moss was not lingering any longer. He was already sprinting to the boat, beginning to climb in. Behind me, I saw my first glimpse of a body through the trees. More

angry, vicious men shouting. I ran, too.

Over my shoulder, I saw Tiny. He was nearly hidden in his dark cloak behind a brushy tree. But I knew he was watching to see me climb safely aboard. I just made it as two white men broke the trees, a bloodhound at their heels.

They all came howling toward the water.

The boat shoved off though. Four men, some white and some black, were already paddling faster than I was able to believe. When I looked back to shore, there was no sign of Tiny anywhere.

Two men onshore were about as crazed as a couple of **rabid** dogs. Could've been foaming at the mouth, they were so mean and

In 1859, a white man named John Brown tried to start an uprising of slaves, but he was arrested and hanged.

36

wild. They were aiming at us with two big guns, but not a single shot hit the boat at all. Shouting, too. Running along the bank like they were searching for some boat of their own to catch up with us mid-river.

Our boat just kept moving across the water. Four big men working the oars hard, with faces calm as can be. Determined, too. Looking at them gave me a bit of my own calm, thinking maybe Moss and I were truly in good hands and near to safety.

I breathed in a big gulp of air and hugged my satchel close to me. The hard, firm shape of my drinking gourd pressed against me. I pulled it out, smoothed my hand over Pappy's beautiful carving like it was my lucky charm.

"Look here," I said to Moss. He nodded like he greatly appreciated seeing what he'd only felt in the dark before then.

"Drinking gourd's going to carry us away," he said.

I leaned over and dipped my hand in the cold river water, scooping some into the drinking gourd. Moss understood. I'd already told him about my idea of floating flowers in it.

"Found something along the wood path last night," he said and dug in his pocket. Then he pulled out a stem of **honeysuckle.** It was crumpled a bit but still so sweet smelling it might have just been plucked. I took his offering and floated the little stem of yellow blossoms in the Ohio River water that sloshed around in my drinking gourd. For the first time ever, I could sense a sweetness in my own life. We rocked on toward the new shore, every minute getting closer.

After a while, I couldn't help myself, felt like my eyes wouldn't stay open another minute. Sleep took me on, and I didn't resist. I just slid along with the river, deep into sleep, rocking on the waters that carried us steadily straight away from the devil's clutch-es. When I opened my eyes again, it would be like coming home.

Abraham Lincoln was president during the Civil War. In 1863, he signed the Emancipation Proclamation, which led to the end of slavery.

Even after slavery ended, it was many years before black Americans had the same rights as white Americans.

This little mouse liked honeysuckle as much as I did.
That sweet-smelling flower was a pretty sight floating in my drinking gourd.

THE HISTORY OF THE
UNDERGROUND RAILROAD

Eleven-year-old Aquila lived during a time of great change in the United States. In 1859, attitudes toward slavery were dividing the country. Many Northern states, believing that slavery was wrong, were outlawing it. Most Southern states, believing that slavery was a necessary part of their way of life, were willing to fight to keep it. In 1861, the divisions between slave states and free states led to the American Civil War (1861–1865).

More than 700,000 slaves lived in the South in the mid-1800s. In Virginia alone, slaves accounted for more than half of the population. Slaves were brought to the American colonies as early as 1619 to work on plantations. The warm climate and fertile soil of the Southern colonies were perfect for growing rice, tobacco, sugar cane, and cotton. Slave traders continued to bring slaves to the United States even after the American Revolution and into the early 1800s.

For two hundred years, the slave trade operated between western Africa and the Americas. Warring tribes from the three wealthy black empires of Ghana, Mali, and Songhai in Western Sudan captured their enemies and traded them for European goods. Europeans in turn sold the slaves to their colonies in North and South America.

In the United States, white abolitionists and free blacks attacked slavery in newspapers and public speeches. They helped between 50,000 and 100,000 runaway slaves travel the Underground Railroad, a system of secret routes leading out of the South. Slaves made the dangerous journey north into Pennsylvania, Ohio, and Canada. At night, they followed the Big Dipper (the Drinking Gourd), which pointed to Polaris, the bright North Star that kept them on a northerly course even in darkness.

When runaways crossed the Ohio River, which divided slave states and free states, they expected to be free. Unfortunately, it took another hundred years before blacks experienced the same freedoms and rights as other Americans. In the 1960s, Aquila's great-grandchildren would reap the benefits of her brave struggles to be free.

GLOSSARY

abolitionist a person who favored an end to slavery in the United States before the Civil War

acclimatize to get used to a new place or situation

anvil a heavy iron block on which metal is shaped

auction a type of sale made to the highest bidder

Big Dipper a group of seven stars that look like a ladle in outline; they are found in the northern part of the sky

bondage slavery, lack of freedom

brand a mark made by burning with a hot iron

broadcloth a fabric with a dense texture

colored an out-of-date term for African-American or black

commotion noisy confusion

conductor a person who works on a train and helps passengers

crescent the shape of the moon when less that half of it is visible

dank unpleasantly moist or sweet

TIMELINE

1638 The New England slave trade begins in Boston, Massachusetts.

1734 The Great Awakening (a major religious movement in early America) begins in Massachusetts. The movement spreads to other areas, encouraging new religious fervor among both blacks and whites. This movement encourages blacks to join the Methodist and Baptist Churches.

1750s—early 1800s Black preachers minister to free and enslaved blacks. Small, independent, black congregations begin to emerge in the south.

1776 The Declaration of Independence is signed. The document causes politicians to rethink slavery, but it is not abolished.

1793 The Fugitive Slave Act is signed, outlawing any efforts to interfere with the capture of runaway slaves in the United States.

fortunate good or lucky

gourd a fruit, like a pumpkin or squash, with a hard skin, often carved and used for decoration or as a utensil

hemp a tall herb with a tough base fiber, often used to make rope

honeysuckle a flower with showy blossoms and rich in nectar

huffy irritated, offended because of pride

ornery bad-tempered or stubborn

plantation a large piece of land used for farming and often worked by hired help or slaves

Polaris another name for the North Star, which is the star in the northern hemisphere toward which the axis of the earth points

rabid extremely violent, as though infected with rabies

satchel a small sack or bag, often with a shoulder strap

Underground Railroad a system run by antislavery workers who helped slaves escape to the northern United States or Canada

1827 The first African-American newspaper, *Freedom's Journal,* begins publication in New York.

1831 Nat Turner, a Baptist slave preacher, leads a revolt in Southampton County, Virginia, killing at least fifty-seven whites.

1849 Harriet Tubman escapes slavery and later returns south at least fifteen times to help rescue several hundred others.

1857 On March 6, the U.S. Supreme Court decides that an African-American cannot be a citizen of the United States and has no rights of citizenship.

1859 The *Clothilde,* the last slave ship to bring slaves to the United States, lands in Mobile Bay, Alabama.

1860 On November 6, Abraham Lincoln is elected the sixteenth president of the United States.

1861 The Civil War begins.

1863 The Emancipation Proclamation takes effect January 1, legally freeing slaves in areas of the South.

1865 The Civil War ends, and the Thirteenth Amendment outlaws slavery in the United States.

ACTIVITIES

Continuing the Story *(Writing Creatively)*

Continue Aquila's story. Elaborate on an event from her scrapbook or add your own entries to the beginning or end of her journal. You might write about Aquila's life as a slave on Oak Rest Plantation before she was separated from her family. Or you can write about her life as a freed slave living in the North. You can also write your own short story of historical fiction based on slavery in the southern United States during the 1860s.

Celebrating Your Heritage *(Discovering Family History)*

Research your own family history. Find out if you had any relatives living in the United States in the 1860s. Were they living in the North or in the South? Ask family members to write down what they know about people and events during this time period. Were any of your relatives involved directly or indirectly with slavery or the Underground Railroad? Explain. Make copies of old photographs or drawings of keepsakes from this time period.

Documenting History *(Exploring Community History)*

Find out how your city or town was affected by slavery and the Underground Railroad in the 1860s. Visit your library, historical society, museum, or local Web site for links to these events. What did the newspapers report? When, where, why, and how did your community take action to support slavery and destroy the Underground Railroad or support the Underground Railroad and free the slaves? Who was involved? What was the result?

Preserving Memories *(Crafting)*

Make a scrapbook about family life in the United States in the 1860s. Imagine what life was like for your family or for Aquila. Fill the pages with special events, family stories, interviews with relatives, letters, and drawings of family treasures. Add copies of newspaper clippings, photos, postcards, birth certificates, slave ownership papers, and historical records. Decorate the pages and the cover with family symbols or slave drawings of drinking gourds, stars in the night sky, and maps of the Underground Railroad routes.

TO FIND OUT MORE

At the Library

Gorrell, Gina K. *North Star to Freedom: The Story of the Underground Railroad.*
New York: Delacorte, 1997.

Hamilton, Virginia. *Many Thousand Gone: African Americans from Slavery to Freedom.*
New York: Knopf, 2002.

Rappaport, Doreen. *Escape from Slavery: Five Journeys to Freedom.*
New York: HarperCollins Juvenile, 1991.

Wyeth, Sharon Dennis. *Freedom's Wings: Corey's Diary, Kentucky to Ohio, 1857.*
New York: Scholastic, 2001.

On the Internet

Aboard the Underground Railroad
www.cr.nps.gov/nr/travel/underground
For information about the historic sites used for the Underground Railroad

The Life of Harriet Tubman
www.nyhistory.com/harriettubman/life.htm
To learn about this remarkable woman and her work

National Geographic: The Underground Railroad
www.nationalgeographic.com/features/99/railroad
To take a virtual journey on an escape to freedom

On the Road

Buxton National Historic Site and Museum
North Buxton, ON
Canada N0P 1Y0
519/352-4799
To visit a settlement that was home to many escaped slaves

National Underground Railroad Museum
115 East Third Street
Maysville, KY 41056
606/564-6986
A museum dedicated to the history of the
Underground Railroad

Through the Mail

The Harriet Tubman Home
180 South Street
Auburn, NY 13201
315/252-2081
To find out more about the life of this
famous abolitionist

A B O U T   T H E   A U T H O R

Pamela Dell has worked as a writer in many different fields, but what she likes best is inventing characters and telling their stories. She has published fiction for both adults and kids, and in the last half of the 1990s helped found Purple Moon, an acclaimed interactive multimedia company that created CD-ROM games for girls. As writer and lead designer on Purple Moon's award-winning "Rockett" game series, Pamela created the character Rockett Movado and twenty-nine others, and wrote the scripts for each of the series' four episodic games. Purple Moon's website, which was based on these characters and their fictional world of Whistling Pines, went on to become one of the largest and most active online communities ever to exist on the Net. Pamela lives in Santa Monica, California, where her favorite fun is still writing fiction and creating cool interactive experiences.